THE THREE BILLY GOATS GRUFF

W9-CHA-234

Dona Herweck Rice

Editorial Director
Dona Herweck Rice

Assistant Editors
Leslie Huber, M.A.
Katie Das

Editor-in-Chief
Sharon Coan, M.S.Ed.

Editorial Manager
Gisela Lee, M.A.

Creative Director
Lee Aucoin

Illustration Manager/Designer
Timothy J. Bradley

Illustrator
Rick Reason

Publisher
Rachelle Cracchiolo, M.S.Ed.

Teacher Created Materials
5301 Oceanus Drive
Huntington Beach, CA 92649-1030
http://www.tcmpub.com
ISBN 978-1-4333-0166-7
© 2008 Teacher Created Materials, Inc.

The Three Billy Goats Gruff

Story Summary

Three billy goats live in a valley. One billy goat is small. One billy goat is big. And one billy goat is in the middle.

The valley is next to a green meadow. A blue river flows between the valley and the meadow. A stone bridge crosses the river. But a mean troll lives under the bridge. The troll wants to eat the goats.

The grass in the meadow grows long and thick. The billy goats want to eat the grass. But they must cross the bridge to get there. The billy goats are smart, and they are strong, too. Will they find a way to cross the bridge? Read the story to find out.

Tips for Performing
Reader's Theater

Adapted from Aaron Shepard

- Don't let your script hide your face. If you can't see the audience, your script is too high.

- Look up often when you speak. Don't just look at your script.

- Talk slowly so the audience knows what you are saying.

- Talk loudly so everyone can hear you.

- Talk with feelings. If the character is sad, let your voice be sad. If the character is surprised, let your voice be surprised.

- Stand up straight. Keep your hands and feet still.

- Remember that even when you are not talking, you are still your character.

- Narrator, be sure to give the characters enough time for their lines.

Tips for Performing
Reader's Theater *(cont.)*

- If the audience laughs, wait for them to stop before you speak again.

- If someone in the audience talks, don't pay attention.

- If someone walks into the room, don't pay attention.

- If you make a mistake, pretend it was right.

- If you drop something, try to leave it where it is until the audience is looking somewhere else.

- If a reader forgets to read his or her part, see if you can read the part instead, make something up, or just skip over it. Don't whisper to the reader!

- If a reader falls down during the performance, pretend it didn't happen.

The Three Billy Goats Gruff

Characters

Narrator	Billy Goat 3
Billy Goat 1	Bridge
Billy Goat 2	Troll

Setting

This reader's theater takes place in a valley. A river runs through it. There is a bridge to take you across the river. A meadow is on the other side of the bridge.

Act 1

Narrator:	The sun shines on a pretty valley. It is the home of three billy goats. Their last name is Gruff.
Billy Goat 1:	*(in a high voice)* Ma-a-a-a!
Billy Goat 2:	*(in a medium voice)* Ma-a-a-a!
Billy Goat 3:	*(in a very deep voice)* Ma-a-a-a!
Troll:	And me. Do not forget about me!
Narrator:	Oh, yes. A troll also lives in the valley. It is a mean and nasty troll.

Troll: A good troll *is* mean and nasty.

Narrator: Hush now! This is not your story. This is the story of the three billy goats Gruff.

Troll: Bah! Who wants to hear about billy goats? I will eat any billy goat who tries to cross my bridge!

Bridge: Leave me out of it! I am a nice bridge. I do not want any trouble.

Narrator: Will you both be quiet, please? I would like to tell the story.

Bridge: Sorry.

Troll: Bah!

Narrator: I will begin again. There are three
                  billy goats. They live in a valley.

Billy Goat 1: I am the smallest billy goat. I am just
                  a kid.

Billy Goat 2: I am not small. I am not big either. I
                  am medium.

Billy Goat 3: Well, I am big. I am strong, too. Can
                  you see my big horns?

Narrator: The three billy goats are playing in
                  the sun. But they stop their play.
                  They are getting hungry. They want
                  to eat.

Billy Goat 1: Oh, I am so hungry. I want to eat some tall green grass.

Billy Goat 2: The best grass is over there. It is in the meadow.

Billy Goat 3: We must cross the bridge to get there!

Billy Goat 1: The bridge? Do you mean the stone bridge? The one the troll lives under?

Billy Goat 2: Yes, that is the one.

Billy Goat 3: It is the only bridge. There is no other way to get to the tall green grass.

Billy Goat 1: I am not afraid! I will cross the bridge. Just watch me!

Song: London Bridge

Act 2

Narrator: The little billy goat walks to the bridge. He puts one hoof on it. Then he puts another. Then he steps all the way on the bridge.

Billy Goat 2: Be careful!

Billy Goat 3: Oh, I can't watch!

Bridge: Trip, trap, trip, trap. Someone is walking across me. Trip, trap, trip, trap.

Troll: Who is walking across my bridge?

Billy Goat 1: It is I, the smallest billy goat.

Bridge: Trip, trap, trip, trap. What a nice sound that is!

Troll: I will eat you, billy goat!

Bridge: Do be careful, little goat!

Billy Goat 1: You do not want me, troll. I am too small. Wait for the next billy goat. He is bigger than I am. There will be more for you to eat.

Troll: More, you say? I am very hungry. All right. You can cross my bridge. Eat a lot of grass and get fat. I will eat you when you come back!

Narrator: So the small billy goat runs far away. Go, goat, go!

Bridge: Trip, trap, trip, trap, trip, trap!

Billy Goat 1: What a silly troll! Now I am safe. I can eat all I want.

Poem: Jack Sprat

Billy Goat 2: Did you see that? The kid made it! I am hungry. I will try to cross the bridge, too.

Billy Goat 3: Be careful! That troll also looks hungry.

Narrator: The billy goat steps on the bridge.

Bridge: Trip, trap, trip, trap. Someone is walking across me. Trip, trap, trip, trap.

Troll: Who is walking across my bridge?

Billy Goat 2: It is I, the medium billy goat.

Bridge: Trip, trap, trip, trap. I am so glad you are visiting me. But the troll is in a nasty mood. Watch your step!

Troll: I will eat you, billy goat! I know that you are fatter than the little goat.

Billy Goat 2: You do not want me, troll. I am too small. The next billy goat is the biggest of all. He is bigger than the kid. He is bigger than me. You will be glad you waited for him.

Troll: I am very, very hungry. I can eat a very large goat. All right. You can cross my bridge. Eat a lot of grass and get fat. I will eat you when you come back!

Narrator: So the medium goat runs far away. Go, goat, go!

Bridge: Trip, trap, trip, trap, trip, trap!

Billy Goat 2: What a silly old troll! Now I can also eat all the grass I want.

Billy Goat 1: I knew you could do it!

Billy Goat 2: Ma-a-a-a! Let's eat!

Act 3

Narrator: The biggest goat is hungry, too. He likes the look of the tall green grass.

Billy Goat 3: The smallest goat made it across. The medium goat made it across. I am the biggest goat. I am the smartest goat. I am the strongest goat, too. I can walk across that bridge!

Narrator: With that, the billy goat steps on the bridge.

Bridge: Trip, trap, trip, trap. Someone is walking across me. Trip, trap, trip, trap.

Troll: Who is walking across my bridge?

Billy Goat 3: It is I, the biggest billy goat.

Bridge: Trip, trap, trip, trap. My, you are a big fellow. You make a loud noise. Trip, trap, trip, trap!

Troll: I will eat you, billy goat!

Narrator: The biggest billy goat lies to the troll.

Billy Goat 3: You do not want me, troll. I am not very big at all. There are many billy goats who are bigger than me.

Troll: You can not fool me! I know that you are big. I know that you are the biggest billy goat.

Billy Goat 1: Oh, I think he is in trouble.

Billy Goat 2: It does not look good for him now.

Billy Goat 3: All right. That is true. I am the biggest. But I am also the smartest.

Troll: You are not smarter than me! I know that I can catch you. I know that I can eat you.

Billy Goat 3: Yes, you can eat me if you catch me. But you can not catch me.

Troll: Why not? I am a troll. I am mean. I am strong. Here I come!

Narrator: The troll leaps. He leaps up from below the bridge. He leaps at the biggest billy goat.

Bridge: Help! Help! I do not want trouble!

Troll: I am going to eat you, billy goat!

Billy Goat 3: Oh, no, you are not!

Narrator: With that, the biggest billy goat leaps at the troll. His head is down. His horns are up.

Troll: Oooowwww!

Billy Goat 3: Take that, troll!

Narrator: The billy goat pushes the troll. The troll falls in the river. Splash!

Bridge: Goodbye!

Narrator: They do not see the troll again.

Billy Goat 3: The troll will not eat today. But I will!

Narrator: The goat walks across the bridge.

Bridge: Trip, trap, trip, trap. My, that has a nice sound!

Narrator: He joins the other billy goats. He will eat all the tall green grass that he wants.

Billy Goat 1: I knew that you could do it. Ma-a-a-a!

Billy Goat 2: Dig in, my friend! Ma-a-a-a!

Billy Goat 3: It is good to be a billy goat! Ma-a-a-a!

Narrator: And maybe not so good to be a troll.

Jack Sprat

Traditional

Jack Sprat could eat no fat.
His wife could eat no lean.
And so between the two of them
They licked the platter clean.

Jack ate all the lean.
Joan ate all the fat.
The bone they picked it clean,
Then gave it to the cat.

 # London Bridge

Traditional

London Bridge is falling down,
Falling down, falling down.
London Bridge is falling down,
My fair lady.

Build it up with needles and pins,
Needles and pins, needles and pins.
Build it up with needles and pins,
My fair lady.

Pins and needles rust and bend,
Rust and bend, rust and bend.
Pins and needles rust and bend,
My fair lady.

Build it up with silver and gold,
Silver and gold, silver and gold.
Build it up with silver and gold,
My fair lady.

Gold and silver I have none
I have none, I have none.
Gold and silver I have none,
My fair lady.

Glossary

billy goat—a male goat

dig in—eat all you want

fool—trick

kid—a young goat

ma-a-a-a—the sound a goat makes

meadow—grassland

troll—a mean and nasty creature who lives in caves or below ground

valley—flat or low land at the bottom of a hill or mountain